BETTER BY MYLES

By

Mark Stretton

Published by new Generation Publishing in 2023,
Copyright © Mark Stretton 2023

First Edition

The author asserts the moral right under the Copyright,
Designs and Patent Act 1988 to be identified as the author
of this work.

All rights reserved. No part of this publication may be
reproduced, stored in a retrieval system or transmitted, in
any form or by any means without the prior consent of the
author, nor be otherwise circulated in any form of binding
or cover other than that which it is published and without
a similar condition being imposed on the subsequent
purchaser.

ISBN
    Paperback 978-1-83563-027-3

www.newgeneration-publishing.com

Author's Note

Better by Myles is entirely a work of fiction.

I have tried to make this story appear more authentic by including real locations, actual events, facts and names of people both alive and dead. I hope I have not offended them or their descendants.

CONTENTS

Chapter 1   The Trust 5

Chapter 2   Fishing 17

Chapter 3   Rise and Fall 23

Chapter 4   The Scam 27

Chapter 5   Hobson's Choice 32

Chapter 6   Oil 38

Chapter 7   Threats 52

Chapter 8   Modus Operandi 57

Chapter 9   The Swimming Pool 59

Chapter 10 Investigations 62

Chapter 11 The Ritz 69

Chapter 12 Locked Up 74

Chapter 13   Transition 85

Chapter 14 More Myles 88

Better by Myles

Chapter 1
The Trust

I hardly knew Myles Horton-McDowd, yet he shaped my career and was responsible for my good fortune.

He was the second son of Sir James Horton-McDowd the brewer, with public houses throughout the Midlands and Southern England. After Myles graduated from Cambridge, he took a year off to travel to the Far East and Australia, and on his return, his father and elder brother welcomed him into the company. He spent several months familiarising himself with the brewery until his father thought that he was ready for a more important role.

Several of their public houses had accommodation and Sir James asked Myles to visit all those with more than eight bedrooms to see whether they were of a sufficient standard to be marketed as a branded hotel group under the name of Horton Inns.

Myles enjoyed this job. Most of the pubs were managed or tenanted by married couples and, however far away, Myles would endeavour to arrive at the property in the late morning. He was always warmly welcomed and after lunch he would spend the afternoon looking at the accommodation. He made copious notes as to the suitability of the bedrooms, their situation and whether they were ensuite or could be made ensuite. He was extremely conscientious.

He would spend most of the evening in the bar, where his good looks and personality would endear him to all he met, particularly the ladies. He bought drinks for those he talked to and retired to bed happy and slightly drunk. In the morning he would check out, request his bill for his accommodation and food and then, in his usual charming way, ask the tenants or managers to settle it for him, which they invariably did.

When he got back to the office, he would give his bill and the notes of his visit to his secretary, who would claim his expenses and write up his notes.

This all went well until he visited The Stag at Enfield. The landlord, David Wright, had a very attractive eighteen-year-old daughter. David let her work in the bar on the condition that she did not drink. As usual, Myles spent the evening in the bar socialising with customers and buying them drinks. Every time Myles bought a round of drinks, he would flirtingly say to the daughter, "Have one for yourself." She always refused.

When the bar closed, Myles helped clear up and went to his bedroom. He did not have time to remove his jacket before there was a knock on the door. The attractive daughter pushed past him, threw herself on the bed and hugging her knees, laughingly said, "I'll have that drink now."

Myles didn't have time to shut the door before a very angry father pushed him into the room, saying, "Leave my daughter alone." He grabbed the girl and dragged her out. Myles thought no more about it and the following morning settled his bill in the usual way with the landlady and left.

The following day his father summoned him into his office. Evidently, the landlord of The Stag had telephoned the company secretary to complain that Myles had invited his daughter into his bedroom and tried to seduce her. Furthermore, Myles had failed to pay his bill. When the company secretary investigated, it became clear that Myles never paid the bill, but always claimed expenses. Over time, this had amounted to quite a lot of money.

There was a joke in the pub trade about the pub manager who fainted outside the bank when he discovered that he had, by mistake, banked the fiddle and kept the takings. Sir James, aware of the number of fiddles in the pub industry, had made it company policy that anyone proved to be dishonest was sacked. He had no choice, and it was decided that Myles should leave.

Of course, he wasn't just fired. For some time, Sir James had been planning to set up an investment trust, primarily to invest his own great wealth but also to attract other investors. His old friend Todd Benson, a chartered accountant and experienced investment banker, had been engaged to lead this venture, which was to be called the Horton-McDowd Investment Trust. Myles was appointed to the board.

Their timing could not have been better. The 1960s had started badly for investors. A joke made the rounds in America that J F Kennedy had tried to reassure a businessman by saying, "Things look great. Why, if I wasn't president, I'd be buying stock myself."
The businessman replies, "If you weren't president, so would I."

However, from 1962 the stock market flourished.

To everyone's surprise Myles and Todd worked very well together and they made cautious yet astute investments in quoted companies. The Horton-McDowd Investment

Trust, or HMIT as it was known, quickly became successful and respected in the city.

Two years later, having established his reputation, Myles persuaded Todd to be more adventurous and buy into non-quoted companies.

His very first investment came about by a chance meeting at the Royal Automobile Club in Pall Mall. He struck up a conversation with an elderly member called Frank Gates, who, it turned out, was the principal of a Ford main dealership on the north-eastern edge of London.

"I guess business is good." Myles ventured.

"Very good." The member replied. "That's half the trouble."

He went on to explain that his dealership was so successful that Ford was pressuring him to build a large new dealership on the edge of town, and while he agreed with Ford, that it would be a good investment, he was bemoaning the fact that it had come at the wrong time of his life.

Both his children had successful careers, and neither was interested in joining the dealership, and he was looking to retire. He was reluctant to raise the extra capital that would be required to expand his dealership. He was also troubled that, some years earlier, he had recruited an excellent young man from Mann Egerton, who was now a director, capable of running the company and was motivated by the prospect of this major expansion.

At this Myles pricked up his ears. There was no way in which he wanted to get involved with running a Ford main dealership. He would be reluctant even to drive a Ford, but, with management in place, this might be a good investment. They exchanged business cards.

Within six weeks HMIT had acquired the dealership and nearly two years later, on 17th June 1966, to much fanfare, the new showroom and workshops were opened. That weekend, Ford won the Le Mans 24-hour race.

Myles kept his eye open for other investment opportunities and shortly after the acquisition of the dealership, another came his way. Admiral Brooke was a member of his livery company. He was one of the Navy's youngest admirals, attached to the Ministry of Defence and, Myles thought rather full of his own importance. Myles generally avoided him, but at the pre-dinner drinks, Myles found himself alone with Admiral Brooke, who, with his usual capacity to blow his own trumpet, was explaining how important he was.

"You have no idea of the bureaucracy at the Ministry. Do you know there are seven separate departments that I have to consult?"

Myles nodded distractedly, looking over the Admiral's shoulder for someone more interesting to talk to, but he maintained his instinct to listen.

"The private sector's fine," continued the Admiral. "They're raring to go. It's a big order for them. Four training vessels, and it's all held up by the Ministry. The department that's responsible for kitchen hygiene or some such thing."

Another member joined them, and the conversation turned to other things.

It was not until Myles was in the office the next day that he recalled his conversation with the Admiral. He wondered which shipyard was going to get the order for the training vessels. Would they make money out of the contract? Was there an opportunity here? Perhaps he ought to investigate.

Myles' friends would have described him as confident, adventurous and cavalier, yet in one respect, at least, he was punctilious. Since his school days, he had kept an address book. The book had changed several times over the years, but Myles was fastidious about carrying forward his contacts into his new book. Shortly after he joined HMIT, he was in despair when he thought he had lost this precious book.

Fortunately, the landlord of the Antelope found it and returned it by post. Myles gave it to Joy, his secretary, who typed out all the entries and filed them carefully in alphabetical order in a ring binder so that he would never lose the contents of his address book ever again. Every Tuesday Myles handed over his personal address book to Joy, who typed up her copy.

Myles knew that Katherine would be in his address book. She was a friend, of about his age, whom he had met several times. Her father was one of the country's largest civil engineers, but Myles seemed to remember that he also owned a shipyard. Sure enough, Katherine was in his address book under "D" for "Dowsett."

After the usual pleasantries and catching up on past times, Myles asked, "Am I right that your father owns a shipyard?"

"Yes." Katherine replied. "Why do you ask?"

Myles explained and asked Katherine whether she knew if their yard was building four vessels for the Ministry of Defence.

"I've no idea. Bill Prouten is the managing director. Ask him. Just tell him you spoke to me."

His next call was to Bill Prouten. Myles was worried whether his questions about navy vessels flouted official secret legislation, but Bill was helpful and assured him that the whole project had gone out to tender some two years before and, although the details of design might be secret, the tendering process had been public. Their yard had been busy at the time, and they had decided not to quote. He believed the contract had gone to Fielding and Marsh on the Tyne. Myles was disappointed that they had decided not to quote.

"Aren't these MOD contracts profitable then?" Myles asked.

"On the contrary, they're very profitable." Bill replied, "The secret is to have a very efficient estimating department."

"How so?" Myles asked.

"The MOD will make hundreds of changes and if you cost every alteration carefully and profitably, you can make a very great deal of money."

"Why didn't you quote?"

"We would have loved the job, but they insisted that we lay the keel of the first vessel within six months, and we were too busy to guarantee that."

"But that was two years ago."

"I know, but that's typical of the MOD. If Fielding and Marsh did get the work, they will have already added several thousands of pounds for inflation before they even start building. As I say these contracts can be very profitable."

It didn't take long to research Fielding and Marsh. Todd was able to check their filed accounts and Joy rang one of the secretaries at the Newcastle Evening Chronicle. Evidently, Fielding and Marsh were a long-established shipyard, employed a happy workforce of good craftsmen, who had never gone on strike and built excellent ships, such as tugs, coasters, supply vessels, fishing vessels and smaller ships for the Royal Navy.

Todd Benson could not really see the purpose of buying into a shipyard. Shipyards in the UK were in decline, and Todd had always impressed upon Myles the damage that association with failure or even bankruptcy would do to their reputation. But even Todd had to admit that with a full order book, Fielding and Marsh might be a good investment. They had traded profitably over many years, and the assets of the yard had been written down so it was likely that the business could be bought relatively cheaply.

The shares had been held equally by Frank Fielding and Henry Marsh until a few years earlier when a Michael Marsh had become a director holding 20% of the shares and both John and Henry had reduced their holding to 40%. John Fielding was 58, Henry was 54 and Michael, who had a degree, was about the same age as Myles. It was agreed that Myles would investigate further.

Myles always preferred the direct approach. He telephoned the yard and asked to speak to Michael. He explained that he was a director of an investment trust and that they were considering investing in Fielding and Marsh. He would like to keep this approach confidential for the time being. Could they meet?

They met the following week in the lounge of the Royal Station Hotel in Newcastle. Myles took to Michael immediately. Michael explained that he had graduated from the London School of Economics and stayed on, enjoying the life of academia, until a couple of years ago, when he had received an urgent call to say that his father was ill. Michael had returned to the Tyne and become involved in the shipyard.

Both Frank and Henry had persuaded him to stay and had given him twenty per cent of the company. Michael told Myles, on a confidential basis, that he had no long-term desire to remain at the shipyard. His strategy, which he had discussed with the other directors, was to secure the contract for the training vessels and sell the yard together with the contracts as soon as possible.

"How positive are you that you will get the contract?" Myles asked.

"I think it's certain. They've told us that the vessels are going to Swansea, Bristol, Liverpool and Cardiff as training vessels for the RNVR and that they are looking forward to commissioning them."

"So, once you get the contract, you will try to find a buyer for the yard?"

"Yes." Michael answered, "I think that would be the best possible exit route for me, my father and Frank."

This strategy interested Myles, so he asked the obvious question.

"I suppose that means that none of you would be interested in selling shares at this stage."

"I very much doubt it." Michael replied.

Myles returned to London thinking that he had had a wasted journey, but a few days later he received a call from Frank Fielding. He was prepared to consider an offer for his shares.

Evidently, over many years, Frank had built up a large portfolio of rental properties in the Newcastle area. One of Frank's associates was a local builder, who had nearly completed a block of eight flats in the Fenham area of Newcastle. He had run out of money and was prepared to sell the block to Frank at a very good price if Frank financed its completion. To finance the deal, Frank would consider selling his interest in Fielding and Marsh.

He had given his fellow directors first refusal but they both agreed that they would like HMIT to take over the shares. It didn't take long to agree a price. HMIT bought forty per cent of the shipyard and Myles became a director.

The yard was building two trawlers for Boston Deep Sea Fisheries. One was nearing completion and the other, the Boston Wayfarer, was to be launched within a matter of weeks. Michael thought that it would be a good idea if Myles were to attend the launch.

The launch was a very jolly affair. The naming was carried out by one of Sir Fred Parkes' granddaughters and there were no fewer than eleven members of the family present. The Boston Wayfarer was to be based at Lowestoft so Bill Suddaby, the manager of their Lowestoft fleet, was also there. Bill was a large well-built friendly man, who made Myles welcome and introduced him to the family. Myles particularly liked Sir Fred Parkes. He was dressed immaculately and covered in some expensive cologne. He evidently enjoyed his success and was happy to tell Myles about some of his ventures.

Only two weeks after the launch, following a review by the Secretary of State for Defence, the Wilson government decided to make significant reductions in the defence budget. Two weeks later, the contract for the training vessels was cancelled.

This was a disaster for Fielding and Marsh and an emergency meeting was called to consider what the future held for the shipyard. At the meeting Henry and Michael explained to Myles that they had been concentrating on the order for the Ministry of Defence to such an extent that they had not pursued other contracts. Their order book was empty, and it would take some time to find other work. They had about eight months' work for their fitters, electricians, shipwrights and joiners but only four months' work for their boilermakers and welders before they would have to start laying them off.

"Why don't you just build another Boston Wayfarer?" asked Myles.

Michael smiled, but this father said, "That's not such a silly idea. I believe Ulstein in Norway build supply ships on a production line basis, but it wouldn't work for the British fishing industry."

He went on to explain that the British fishing fleet had been built up with the help of grants from the government, special loans if they built their vessels in the UK and operating subsidies.

"Besides, every owner has his own ideas about design. The Wayfarer was built largely for one of Boston's top skippers, Ray Prior, who specialises in catching cod. If we built another Wayfarer, it probably wouldn't appeal to another owner. It's just not possible."

Jokingly Myles said, "What you would like me to do is start a fishing company and give you an order for four large trawlers."

They laughed.

Chapter 2 Fishing

As Myles sat in his first-class carriage on the long journey back to London, he wondered whether his jokey comment was so stupid. Fielding and Marsh faced closure.

Bankruptcy could probably be avoided as eventually the assets and the yard would be sold, but there would be a huge write-down on the value of the shares held by HMIT.

Only an order to build another ship would save the shipyard and Myles began to consider whether he might venture into the fishing industry so that he could place an order for a new trawler. Bill Suddaby and the Parkes family seemed to epitomise the same sort of buccaneering attitude as his own, and he did not mind admitting that the fishing industry attracted him. Farming, mining and fishing were primary industries and with the additional attraction of the sea and the excitement of the hunt, deep sea fishing appealed.

At the office, the next day he told Todd of the problems at Fielding and Marsh, but thought it was too early to broach the possibility of buying into the fishing industry. He wanted to carry out a little more research first. His first impulse was to ring Bill Suddaby at Lowestoft, but he hesitated. He couldn't rationalise his hesitation. It was partly not to appear foolish and partly because he knew that, if anything came of his plans, Bill Suddaby and the Parkes family would want too much involvement.

He wondered whether Lowestoft was the right location for a venture into the fishing industry, but Bill had painted such a rosy picture of the port's prosperity that he didn't seriously consider anywhere else. Besides, Lowestoft was closest. He decided to visit the port.

According to the AA handbook, there were four hotels of any size in Lowestoft, the Royal, the Victoria, the Hatfield and the Suffolk Hotel. The first three were located near the Esplanade and were clearly for holiday makers, so he booked a room at the Suffolk Hotel.

As he crossed the square from Lowestoft railway station to the hotel, he could see the masts of fishing vessels moored in the Trawl Dock. There was a prosperous-looking department store opposite him, and two well-built young men passed him, one wearing a black suit with red lapels and pocket flaps, the other in a mustard-coloured suit with a black martingale and lapels. It was early evening and there was a gentle sea breeze. After London, everything seemed cleaner and fresher.

Not so his hotel. It was old, tired and run down. The basin in his room was cracked and the bathroom was down a dark corridor. He decided to explore the town but when he returned to the ground floor, he found that the public bar was open and customers were sitting at rather grubby tables or standing at the bar, including the two young men in the colourful suits. Sitting down at an empty table, Myles asked an elderly man at the next table who the two young men were.

"They're fishermen." replied the man and went on to explain that the deckhands were so prosperous that they could afford to have suits made to measure and that these colourful suits had become the fashion.

Myles spent the whole evening in the bar speaking to more than a dozen fellow customers. Whether it was all true, Myles was not certain, but by the end of the evening he felt he had learnt all there was to learn about the Lowestoft fishing industry and community. He retired to bed slightly drunk but very much the wiser.

Most importantly, he had learnt that there were four main fishing companies, East Coast, Talisman, Boston and Hobsons. East Coast was owned by a very rich man, who lived away and visited his company every week, driving one of his several Ferraris. Talisman was a young company and apart from Boston, which he knew about, there only remained the more mature Hobsons. They had been in business for many years.

When he returned to London, he was even more keen to invest in the fishing industry, but now it was not only to save Fielding and Marsh but as a sensible investment opportunity. In order to investigate further, he would have to confide in Todd.

Todd was surprisingly receptive to the idea and together with Joy quickly set about researching Hobsons. Once again Joy contacted the local paper, the Lowestoft Journal, to discover that the paper carried reports on the industry and was able to recommend one or two books on the subject, which she bought. Within ten days they produced a brief well-researched document.

"The Spashett family are the principal owners of Hobsons Ltd. The family moved to Lowestoft in about 1860 when the fishing industry at Barking went into decline, and by the time the second world war broke out, the Spashetts owned or managed 62 fishing vessels. The North Sea was closed for fishing during the war and almost all their fishing vessels were commandeered by the Navy. Since the war, under George Spashett they have built up a modern fleet of 23 fishing vessels. The business is now ninety per cent owned by 62-year-old George Spashett and his four younger sisters. The remaining ten per cent owned by Edward Utting. The company is profitable but since building four stern trawlers has not invested in new vessels for nearly four years'.

Myles and Todd both thought that it would be worth contacting George Spashett to enquire whether he and his sisters might be open to an offer for their shares and decided that a formal written letter signed by Myles, which George could refer to his accountant and his sisters, would probably receive serious consideration.

George's reply was short and equally formal. It suggested a meeting at the Great Eastern Hotel and requested that his fellow director, Edward Utting, also be present.

Events proceeded quickly from that point. Todd, Myles, George and Edward met at the Great Eastern. They all liked each other and enjoyed a good lunch. It was agreed that, on a strictly confidential basis, Todd should visit Lowestoft and talk to Geoffrey Dicker their accountant at Lovewell Blake.

Todd became quite excited when he learnt the extent to which the government supported the fishing industry. Through the White Fish Authority, the government would give a grant of thirty per cent to finance new fishing vessels. The government had also arranged that ICFC, a consortium of the five clearing banks, would give cheap loans of up to sixty per cent of the cost of a new vessel. Furthermore, free depreciation was available on the total cost of a vessel from the tax authorities. Free depreciation

meant that if a company was due to pay corporation tax, it was possible to buy a new fishing vessel and, in cash terms, be better off. This appealed to Todd.
However, if a business did not order a new vessel, corporation tax became due. Hobsons Limited had got into this situation and further investment in new fishing vessels was imperative.

Myles could hardly be bothered with all this. He was more interested in the management of the business. He liked Edward Utting. He was in his fifties, had in the past owned three fishing vessels, knew the industry well and was perfectly capable of taking up the role of managing director of Hobsons. Moreover, he was happy to keep his ten per cent of the company.

Negotiations for the sale of the Spashett holding continued. George knew that his sisters would accept any reasonable offer for their shares and in a very short time, HMIT had acquired ninety per cent of Hobsons Limited.

Such was the excitement of their new acquisition that Todd and Myles had almost forgotten that the original purpose of the purchase was to bail out Fielding and Marsh by ordering fishing vessels from them.

Within weeks they had ordered four very powerful trawlers. They had twin propellors and twin engines, each of one thousand horsepower, and bow thrusters. Myles realised that Fielding and Marsh were deliberately raising the value of Hobsons' order, but he was uncertain as to whose side he was on.

In the spring, the order was signed and the keel of the first stern trawler laid. This followed on immediately from the two Boston trawlers and when the first trawler was delivered to Hobsons, it was clear that Fielding and Marsh were extremely profitable and would be for the foreseeable future.

Michael Marsh had no hesitation in contacting British Shipbuilders to sound them out as to whether they would be interested in the purchase of the shipyard and British Shipbuilders, who were desperate for profits, jumped at the opportunity.

HMIT and Myles were delighted with the profit they made on their shares. Michael's father was equally delighted and retired, and during the negotiations Michael managed to engineer himself an appointment onto the main board of British Shipbuilders. Everyone was happy.

Apart from a Hobsons board meeting every two months, firstly at Lowestoft and later, to save Myles the travel, at the Great Eastern hotel in London, Myles left Edward Utting alone to manage the Lowestoft fleet. The new stern trawlers were very successful.

In any fishing fleet, there is a virtuous circle, in that the best ships attract the best skippers, who attract the best crew. The stern trawlers were the largest and most powerful ships in Lowestoft. They made record catches and earnings. The rest of the Hobsons' fleet also did well, and fishing was extremely profitable. Over the next few years, they sold five of their older vessels and, largely to avoid tax, Hobsons invested in four more stern trawlers.

Chapter 3
Rise and Fall

Throughout the sixties and seventies HMIT's investments rose nearly 500%. Their quoted investments far outperformed the FT30, and their private equity financing was equally satisfactory.

Myles met a Toni Albertini at a charity event in London and immediately offered to finance him and Brett Palos, in a very profitable property business.

Later, on a trip to Leeds he met a successful businessman called George Moore who was in the furniture trade. Myles offered to finance him to develop Thorp Arch, a very successful trading estate.
x
Altogether they had taken a minority interest in 23 different companies, 14 of which, including the first Ford dealership, had either been sold profitably or floated successfully on the stock market.

Myles was in his mid-30s and very well off. He enjoyed life and drank too much. He was still single. In fact, his relationship with the ladies was, to say the least, casual. Most evenings he could be found at either Ronnie Scott's, the Colony Room or The Bag O' Nails.

The staff at HMIT had grown to five, and in 1972 Todd Benson felt that there was enough strength in the management of the business for him to retire. He had invested all his bonuses into HMIT and was able to sell his shares and retire a very wealthy man. Myles was sorry to see him go but HMIT continued to prosper, and Myles began to believe that he had the magic touch.

Hobsons, their fishing company, continued to prosper, but in January 1973, the United Kingdom joined what was then called the Common Market and handed over all fishing rights within their territorial waters to Europe. Norway very sensibly refused to join and maintained their fishing grounds. All our fishing vessels had to have a licence, issued under the Common Fisheries Policy, to fish in waters that we had happily fished before. Perhaps, more importantly, the United Kingdom's Department of Agriculture and Fisheries became almost powerless.

Nobody realised that this inability to support the fishing industry would result in its eventual terminal decline, at least in Hull, Grimsby, Lowestoft, Fleetwood and Aberdeen. This was not surprising as for the first year under the CFP fishing was profitable.

On 6th October 1973, Syria and Egypt launched a surprise attack on Israel. The war lasted until March 1974 and the United States of America decided to support the Israelis. This provoked a united response from the Arab Petroleum Exporting Countries and Egypt, Syria and Tunisia. They flexed their muscles and proclaimed an oil embargo. This raised the price of a barrel of oil from under 20 dollars a barrel to more than 100.

The effect on the stock market was almost catastrophic. Prices dropped by nearly seventy-five per cent and HMIT, who had borrowed extensively, was suddenly in financial difficulties. With hindsight there was never any danger of their going bankrupt, but Myles suddenly faced failure rather than success. He lost any bonus he was due and started to panic. There was not much he could do about the quoted investments, but he ordered a hasty review of those smaller companies in which he had bought equity.

The worst affected of these companies was his fishing company, Hobsons. Not only was the company losing money, but HMIT owned ninety per cent of it. In September 1974, he called an emergency meeting.

Their regular board meetings were held every two months at the Great Eastern hotel. Edward Utting was accompanied by Ivan Dannock, Hobsons' in-house accountant and company secretary. The meeting would start at 11.30 or a little later, depending on the punctuality of their train. Edward and Ivan would arrive to find Myles in the meeting room, drinking a glass of champagne. The meetings were generally brief and were followed by an excellent lunch in the hotel's dining room.

They gathered in the usual room for the emergency meeting. The latest dreadful figures were circulated and discussed. Edward explained that the price of fuel had risen from £13 per ton to £52 per ton and that all the 23 of their trawlers were losing money. Their larger trawlers, with their powerful engines, had been most badly affected.

Myles demanded that the whole fleet immediately cease fishing and be laid up and it took Edward some time to explain that this would increase both the losses and the negative cash flows. A laid-up vessel, he explained, must still be maintained, pay harbour dues and insurance, but more importantly, must continue repaying the loans and the interest on the loans. By continuing fishing, the vessels were still making a small contribution towards these payments.

Myles was frustrated and angry. The Government was apparently unable to help, and the price of fuel could go even higher. Although he didn't say it to Edward and Ivan, he was determined to offload his shares and get out of this loss-making company. It was agreed that they would meet again at their scheduled meeting in October.

Chapter 4
The Scam

After graduating from Thanet Technical College, I joined British Transport Hotels as a trainee manager at the Charing Cross hotel under Mr. Watson. After two years, I transferred to the Great Eastern hotel as an assistant manager, and two years later, I was appointed Banqueting Manager.

Although I oversaw all bookings for banquets, dinner dances and weddings, my role also covered meetings held in the many smaller private rooms. As a matter of procedure, I inspected every room prior to the meeting to ensure that everything was properly set out.

It was in that role that I first met Mr. Horton-McDowd. His company held regular meetings at the hotel. The bookings were always made by a Mr. Dannock from Lowestoft in the name of Hobsons, and I understood that Hobsons was a very successful North Sea fishing company.

As well as the usual bottles of water, a half bottle of Moet et Chandon together with one glass had to be on the table prior to the meeting and when I checked the meeting room, I would invariably find Mr. Horton-McDowd smoking a cigarette and enjoying a glass of champagne.

He always detained me for a chat. He was clearly rich and well connected yet he seemed interested in me, my career and my background. At one of the meetings when a form had to be signed and witnessed, Mr. Horton-McDowd had me paged and asked me to witness a signature. At the

October meeting I found Mr. Horton-McDowd had another gentleman with him. He ordered another half bottle of Moet for the gentleman.

At the meeting Myles introduced the gentleman to Edward and Ivan. He was called Mike Riley and, as Myles explained, he was a man with international connections, particularly in South Africa. He might be able to secure international finance or even a sale of the fishing fleet overseas. Myles asked that he be co-opted to the board of the company and his appointment confirmed at the next Annual General Meeting. In fact, Mike was one of Myles' rather dim but well-connected drinking pals with strict instructions to say nothing at the meetings but to be friendly towards Edward and Ivan over lunch. At the back of Myles' mind was the possibility that he might offload his shares on to Mike.

However, by the December meeting, Myles had other ideas. During our chats I had told Myles that I was brought up as a child in Sri Lanka, that I had fond memories of the country but that my only memento of these happy times was my extensive collection of Sri Lanka and Ceylon postage-stamps, of which I was very proud.

One wet and dismal day in mid-December, Myles was walking in the Strand and passed Stanley Gibbons. In that instant a new plan struck him. He entered the premises and after some discussion bought a Ceylon 1912 one-thousand-rupee stamp for £120.

On his return to the office, he telephoned the Great Eastern and asked to speak to me. When I came to the phone, he explained that he had remembered that I was interested in stamps. He had been looking through his very old collection and had come across a Ceylon 1912 one-thousand-rupee stamp. Would I be interested in buying it? He felt a bit guilty charging me for it but would part with it for £20. If I gave him my address, he would send me the stamp by registered post so that I could check the condition. I could give him a cheque when we met prior to the next meeting. As far as I remembered, this stamp was rare and quite valuable and it would be a marvellous addition to my collection, so I gave him my address and looked forward to receiving the stamp.

Myles' next move was to ring Ivan at Lowestoft to tell him that he had managed to find a buyer for the shares held by HMIT. He would introduce the buyer to both Edward and Ivan at the next meeting and in the meanwhile would Ivan prepare all the documentation and a new share certificate. He gave Ivan the name and address of the buyer.

Myles and Mike arrived for the October meeting a little earlier than usual and Mike was pleased that I had ordered a bottle of Moet for the two of them. I had researched the stamp that he had sent me. It was worth somewhere between £60 and £120, and I told Myles that £20 was too little and offered to pay more. Myles said that he was pleased to encourage me with my collection and that a cheque for £20 would be fine. Would I please make it out to HMIT, and he would get his secretary to pay it into his private account.

At about half past twelve, Myles paged me and asked me to go to the meeting room. He was alone with Mike. He had sent Edward and Ivan to reception so that they could meet and greet the new buyer. There were several documents on the table. Myles and Mike signed them and asked me to witness their signatures. They left the hotel by a side door. Myles was excitedly happy and returned to the office to ensure that my cheque was banked immediately.

Edward and Ivan sat in the reception area for more than 20 minutes waiting for the new buyer.

"Wait here. Perhaps we've missed him. He's probably gone straight to the meeting room." Edward said to Ivan.

Edward found the meeting room empty. His first thought was that Myles and Mike had gone into the restaurant but, when he checked, their usual table was unoccupied. He returned to Ivan in reception.

"They've disappeared!" said Edward.

It was not until they both returned to the meeting room that they discovered that all the paperwork for the sale of ninety per cent of the company to a Mark Stretton had been scrupulously completed.

Immediately, they summoned me to the room.

"Have you seen anyone enter the room?" asked Edward.

"No, no one's been in as far as I know." I replied.

Ivan started examining the paperwork.

"Do you know a Mr. Mark Stretton?" he asked.

"Yes, that's me." I replied.

Ivan looked astonished and showed one of the documents to Edward. He pointed at a signature.

"You've just bought ninety per cent of our business!" exclaimed Edward. "Did you give anyone any money?" he asked.

"No." I replied hesitantly. "I did give Mr, Horton-McDowd a cheque for the stamp."

"How much was it for? he asked. "Who was it made out to?"

"It was for £20." I replied. "Mr Horton-McDowd asked me to make it out to HMIT."

As I related what had happened, it became clear to the three of us that, rather than just witness a signature, I had bought the HMIT's entire holding in Hobsons for £20. Ivan continued to examine the paperwork and held up two sheets of the hotel's letter heading. Both Myles and Mike had resigned from the board of Hobsons.

Chapter 5
Hobson's Choice

The three of us sat down. In nearly seven years I had never sat at the same table as a guest.

"What an idiot!" spluttered Edward, and for a second, I thought he was talking about me. "He just panicked."

"What are you going to do?" Ivan asked looking at me.

I shook my head. "I really don't know. Can you tell me something about the company?"

For the next hour Edward told me all about Hobsons. Ivan kept chipping in and by the time they left to catch the train back to Lowestoft, I was a lot wiser but even more curious.

I always had Sundays off and sometimes Monday as well, so the following day I telephoned Edward and asked if I could travel to Lowestoft on the next Sunday and meet up with him first thing Monday.

"What do you call first thing?" asked Edward and explained that he was always on the fish market at 7.30 every morning, so I agreed to make my own way to the fish market and meet him there. He recommended I stay at the Victoria Hotel and said he would reserve a room for me for Sunday night.

A very pretty receptionist who, according to her name badge, was called Penny, checked me in. It was early afternoon and I decided to walk down the esplanade to the docks and fish market so that I knew where to go the following morning. As I returned to the hotel, it was getting dark and after a drink in a nearly empty bar and dinner in a nearly empty restaurant, I went to bed early.

I reached the fish market at about 7.15 the following morning. Twenty or thirty men in boots and white coats were standing at one end of the dock where the fish from the moored trawler were displayed in aluminium kits. Edward was talking to a man in a white coat, who turned out to be Maurice, Hobsons' auctioneer. Edward greeted me and introduced me to Maurice, but we hardly had time to talk when a young man started ringing a hand bell and Maurice moved off to start the auction. Soon the fish merchants were tallying up their purchases – Mummery, Cole, Easto, Birdseye, Explorator, Evans and many more, all anxious to start the day and contact their customers.

Hobsons had another ship landing that day but after the first auction, Edward suggested we go to the Woodbine Café for some breakfast. Later in Edward's office we discussed whether I wanted a role in the management of Hobsons. I explained that the run up to Christmas at the Great Eastern was my busiest time of year and it was just not possible to walk out on my job.

"With you holding such a huge stake in the company" said Edward "I would be happier if you were here with me."

The company was facing a very difficult time. Bankruptcy was possible and I guess Edward felt that he didn't want to be the only person responsible for the collapse of the business or, more importantly, the loss of the jobs of all those employed.

"May I ask how much you are earning now?" asked Edward.

I told him and he agreed to pay me the same if I moved to Lowestoft and took a job with Hobsons. I learnt later that this was about a quarter of the amount paid to Myles as a director's fee. It was decided that I would give my notice to the Great Eastern and join Hobsons immediately after Christmas.

My introduction to the company was a 12-day trip on a Hobsons' trawler.
The whole Lowestoft fleet had returned to port for Christmas and nearly 120 ships were all sailing following the Christmas break. Edward could have placed me on any of the Hobsons' ships but decided that I would sail on the Suffolk Endeavour under skipper Jackie Soanes.

We steamed for about eight hours to the fishing grounds and shot our net. We hauled every four hours, day and night, for the next 12 days. The crew gutted the fish and stowed the catch in ice in the fish room. Edward had supplied me with suitable fishing gear, and I felt obliged to go on deck to help the crew. I didn't have the skill to gut the fish but was able to pick up the fish and shovel all the seaweed over the side. On one occasion the high-pressure hose was 'accidently' directed in my direction by the third hand, but as the trip progressed the crew appreciated my assistance.

When we returned to port, Edward was on the quay and drove me to a small boarding house, where he had arranged for me to have bed and an evening meal. Breakfast would be at the Woodbine Café. We discussed what we would tell the rest of the staff and decided that at this stage we would let them believe that I was a member of staff at HMIT.

However, within the next few days Edward introduced me to George Mawer, the local Lloyds Bank manager, and we decided that we had to tell him the truth. We met in his office and after explaining the situation, George Mawer looked me up and down and rudely asked, "What do you think you can contribute to this disaster?"

"I have a lot to learn." I replied, "But it seems to me that the most important thing to do is make sure that we reduce our overdraft."

"And how do you think you will do that?" he asked truculently.

"Well." I said, "I've just finished a trip to sea. Everyone worked extremely hard. If fishing doesn't pay, there is something wrong."

"I know that." George scoffed.

"I think we will have to think outside the box and see if there is some other way, we can employ our ships more profitably."

George looked skyward.

Back in the office, Edward thought that I'd handled the interview well.

"George isn't as bad as he seems." he assured me. "But we must keep him on side."

The young man, who had rung the bell prior to the auction was Neil Graves, the second auctioneer. He and Maurice used the board room to calculate the trawler's earnings and prepare the invoices for the fish merchants. There was no office available for me, so Edward had told me to use the board room as my base, and as a result, I soon began helping with the paperwork and would accompany Neil when he delivered the invoices to the fish merchants.

The other staff were all friendly. Barney Smith and Russell Gower were two ex-skippers, who having retired from sea were employed to look after the ships in harbour, making sure that they were ready to sail again. They were called ship's husbands.

Brian was the cashier who calculated the crews' wages and paid them when they came into the office to collect their wages.

The only person who seemed to resent my presence was John Bell, the fleet manager. Apart from Edward and Ivan, all the staff reported to him, and he appointed the skippers and oversaw the safe and efficient operation of the fleet. He was a disciplinarian, and my closeness to the staff and my relationship with Edward and Ivan confused and bothered him.

Otherwise, all was well. My accommodation in the boarding house was adequate, but I was longing to move into my own flat and the evenings were rather dull. One evening I wandered across to the Victoria Hotel in the hope of meeting Penny. The reception desk was empty but when I entered the bar, there she was behind the bar serving drinks to the seven or eight people already there. She greeted me with genuine affection and a smile. The other drinkers gradually left.

"So, you are not just the receptionist?" I asked and she explained that after Burn's night the owners of the hotel took two months off in Tenerife and left her to hold the fort.

I was surprised when she asked, "How are you getting on at Hobsons?"

"How do you know I work there?" I replied.

"My dad's Mr. Utting."

Chapter 6
Oil

Mr. Utting – Edward – would occasionally take me to lunch at the Royal Norfolk and Suffolk Yacht Club. This would confuse and annoy John Bell even more, but it was on one of these occasions that our fortunes changed.

There were two men standing at the bar when we entered. Edward knew one of them and introductions were made. The other person was Ken Davidson. He was the newly appointed manager of Shell and charged with setting up a base at Lowestoft to service the oil exploration that was beginning to take place in the southern North Sea. He was sociable and approachable.

Looking back, I wonder at my naivety, for the following day I wandered down to Shell's base on the north quay and asked the receptionist whether I could see Mr. Davidson. He immediately came into the reception area, recognised me and ushered me into his office and offered me a coffee.

"What can I do for you?" Ken asked.

"I'm not very sure." I replied. "But you mentioned your North Sea operations yesterday and I wondered if we could help."

I explained that Hobsons had been involved in the North Sea for more than 60 years, that we now owned and operated 23 large fishing vessels. Was there any way we could assist?

Ken immediately summoned Dick Kidd into his office and introduced us. Dick oversaw marine operations on the base and Ken suggested that I talk to him.

We went to Dick's office where he explained that they would have two exploration rigs working in the southern North Sea. Legislation required them to have a safety vessel constantly at each rig. The safety vessel had to be large enough to accommodate everybody working on the rig and be on standby in case someone fell from the rig.

"What would you charge to supply a ship?" he asked.

I was quickly getting out of my depth but having been involved with operating a 24-hour service in hotels, I asked the obvious question.

"Would you just need one ship? We would have to bring our vessel back to port for crew changes, refuelling and revictualling." I asked.

Dick thought for a second, then asked, "Would you guarantee 24-four hour a day, 365-day coverage?"

"We would need three ships for that." I replied.

"Can you give me a rough cost?" he asked.

I hesitated, but having helped Maurice calculate the trips, I was able, with more confidence than I felt, to give him a price based on what the ships earnt fishing.

Dick did not give any indication as to whether this was too much, but he did suggest a further meeting.

Edward was delighted with my initiative, but John Bell was clearly cross that I had usurped his authority as fleet manager. It was agreed that I would not be present at the next meeting and that it should be between John and Dick Kidd.

We did some more accurate figures, and I was delighted when the figure I had quoted was adopted. There were several cost savings that I had not considered, such as fishing gear and ice, but most importantly Shell insisted on fuelling our ships at their base and at their cost. Also, I had also not fully considered that we would be paid 365 days a year.

John clearly handled the meeting with Dick well, for within a fortnight, charter documents had been signed and the three ships were converted and ready when Shell's oil rigs started drilling on the 1st of May.

John Bell was entirely responsible for our next change of fortune. He was a member of a shoot and a keen shot and, out of season, practiced skeet shooting. One of his fellow shots was Harry Bark, who, as Bark and Company, had established a well-known and well-respected marine survey business based at Great Yarmouth. Harry was in his late 50s and was recognised by Lloyd's Register, Bureau Veritas and Det Norske Veritas.

Several American oil companies and construction companies had set up in Yarmouth and it was anticipated that American supply vessels would soon follow so when Nigel Mann approached him, Harry, who was a trusting soul, decided to employ him. Nigel, a British man in his early 40s, had worked in the USA for several years based in Port Fourchon on the Gulf of Mexico. He knew the American oil industry, and importantly was recognised by the American Bureau of Shipping. Nigel Mann was very persuasive, and Harry thought that he would be a good addition to his business.

One of Nigel's first initiatives was to contact Grey and Branch, a very large worldwide pipe-lay company that was setting up in Yarmouth. The boss was Rufus Saxton, who had worked for the company for many years all over the world. Wherever he went, Albert Brown went with him. Rufus was the senior and had, in his early days, been master of one of their lay barges. Albert was the fixer. Wherever they worked, Albert could be relied on to get to know the locals and sort out any problems that arose. They were well regarded by Grey and Branch and could be relied on to get the contract completed on time and within budget.

Nigel, with his knowledge of the oil industry, gained from his work in Port Fourchon, was able to establish a rapport with Rufus and Albert, and quickly established that they would require three survey vessels. Nigel asked Harry for advice as to where he could source them.

At the clay pigeon range, Harry asked John Bell whether any of Hobsons' vessels would be available. John thought that the stern trawlers would be ideal for this sort of work and arranged for Harry and Nigel to visit Lowestoft to inspect one of them.

In the event only Nigel turned up. One of the vessels built by Fielding and Marsh was in harbour and John took Nigel aboard to inspect it. Nigel felt that the twin propellors and the bow thruster would make them ideal for the work as occasionally they would have to go alongside the lay barge and manoeuvrability was a great asset. He required that all three were sister ships and John assured him that they would be.

He asked John for an approximate price. The contract was only for six months – the summer months – and John was rather disappointed that the contract was for so short a period. He wondered if it would be worth returning the vessels to fishing just for the winter months, so, for a 6-month contract, John quoted a figure that the trawlers would have earned in a year. Nigel's reaction surprised John.

"That seems fine." Nigel said. "What you don't realise is that the cost of these survey ships is nothing. On a project like this, it's petty cash. Believe me it's more about how you do it than what you charge."

John was mystified, but Nigel continued.

"Rufus and Albert have worked together all over the world. Sometimes in crappy places, where you don't get anywhere without the odd payment or inducement. They know what's what. If I can offer them a small cut, they'll take your ships."

John was excited by this response, but suddenly realised that Edward his boss would never go along with paying bribes and told Nigel so. Nigel laughed.

"Good grief, we wouldn't ask him to do that. I'll talk to Harry and his company, Bark and Co. will just charge a commission. We'll make sure the right people get it. Just add ten per cent to your price to cover commissions. I might be able to deal you in."

John did not report this conversation to anyone. But within two weeks Ivan, Hobsons' company secretary, received three Grey and Branch charter documents from Bark and Company and the price was as exactly what John had quoted, plus ten per cent. There was a separate note from Bark and Co stating that their commission was ten per cent, to be paid into a bank in the Cayman Islands. Ivan was worried and it was with some trepidation that he presented the documents to Edward.

I was with Edward when Ivan drew our attention to the ten per cent commission. We were both concerned about the size of the commission. Normally commissions were one and a quarter per cent for a long-term charter and two and a half per cent for shorter charters. Ten per cent was unheard of. Payment to a bank in the Cayman Islands also caused us some concern. We suspected that Bark and Co was making payments to Rufus and Albert, but eventually, we persuaded ourselves to sign the documents. This was, after all, a very profitable contract.

This contract was a turning point for the company and my circumstances also improved. Edward asked me into his office and told me that he thought I should have a company car. I must admit that inwardly I gave a wry smile as it occurred to me that, as I owned ninety per cent of the company, I might be able to give myself a company car, but my arrangement with Edward worked well and I did not want it to alter. My first company car was a four-year-old Ford Anglia with 44,000 miles on the clock.

Until now I had been lodging in a guest house close to the sea front and walking to the fish market and the office. Most evenings I would wander over to the Victoria hotel for a drink. Of course, the attraction was Penny. During January and February, the hotel was very quiet, and the owners had gone to Tenerife for two months leaving Penny in charge. She would get to work at about noon and work through until eleven o'clock at night, and most evenings Penny covered both the reception and the bar, handing over to the night porter at 11.

I would make my drink last a very long time and when Penny had to work in reception, making up the bills for the following morning, or attending to a customer, I would go behind the bar and help by serving drinks. This was fine until the hotel got busier as summer approached.

I was also getting bored with my boarding house and decided that I would like to get on the property market and buy a flat. Now that I had a car, it could be a mile or two from the fish market and the town. Eventually, I found an excellent two-bedroom flat just off Oulton Road. The purchase price was reasonable and with the help of George Mawer, the bank manager, I was able to arrange the finance. By early summer I had moved in.

My flat was one of six that had been created in a large house originally owned by the Mackintosh family. It was called Brooke House and was set well back from the road. Some of the large garden had been sold off for housing, but the main house was still approached by the original drive. To the right of the drive was a very pleasant and well-kept swimming pool. The pool was about 40 yards from the front door and was enclosed on three sides by a well-established yew hedge. On the sunny side of the pool there was a large patio furnished with chairs and tables and on the south side there were changing rooms next to the car park. As the weather became warmer, the pool became very popular with the occupants of the other flats, who were young couples. Two couples had young children. I saw rather less of Penny as the Victoria hotel was busy, but she usually got Sundays off, and, in good weather, she would come over and have a swim or we would drive out into the country.

At work we were preparing the three stern trawlers for the Grey and Branch contract, and they started working out of Great Yarmouth in the spring. Their role was to carry the surveyors, who would plot the route of the pipeline and lay the buoy pattern for the huge lay barges to follow.

Great Yarmouth was transformed that summer. Apart from Shell, the other oil companies, mostly American, based their operations there. It was not unusual to see Americans in cowboy boots and Stetsons walking down Regent Road.

I was always rather surprised that the famous Great Yarmouth families did not get more involved with the oil industry. Great Yarmouth is so far east, and the roads are so poor that national companies tended to stay away unless they were involved in agriculture like Birdseye or Smiths Crisps. As a result, the success of Great Yarmouth was largely due to entrepreneurs and their families with the famous names of Colton, Botton, Threadwell, Jay, Hardwick, Scott, de Courcy, Mobbs and many others. Apart from, in some cases, benefitting from their custom, these entrepreneurs avoided any direct investment in the oil industry, believing, rightly as it turned out, that it was too temporary.

It was a Lowestoft company R. J. Pryce and Co. who ventured into Great Yarmouth. They were Lowestoft's largest ironmongers based in Suffolk Street with a wholesale department near the Hamilton Dock. They decided to take a 10-year lease on the south quay in Great Yarmouth, where they supplied hardware to the oil industry, who rather disparagingly described them as selling "rope, dope and soap". They employed an experienced American oilman as manager, who negotiated for them to become agents for Whittaker Capsules, which are the large orange escape boats for oil rigs They also took on the agencies for drilling mud and associated products. They were not retailers and did not take cash, but their trade counter did very well.

There were no fewer than 14 supply ships working out of the port and together with diving vessels and survey ships the port was buzzing. Nigel Mann of Bark and Company made it his business to get to know them all. He had a very good relationship with Rufus and Albert, the two Americans who had set up the Yarmouth base for Grey and Branch. Their role was to make sure that nothing stopped the pipe lay barges from laying pipe. The barge masters were paid large bonuses if they achieved their targets and, although Rufus was the boss, he was also the servant of the barge masters to make sure they received all the equipment, spares and maintenance necessary to complete the job efficiently and on time. Nigel, with Harry's local knowledge, became indispensable to Rufus and Albert.

Occasionally, I would also call in to see them. I was careful not to interfere with John's management role, so my visit was nothing more than a courtesy call. They shared a large office, and they were always pleased to see me. I soon learnt that Rufus and Albert and many of their American and UK staff and friends enjoyed a barbecue.

I was rather proud of my new flat, so having consulted Edward and all my neighbours, I asked Rufus whether it would be appropriate for me to host a July 4th barbecue at my new home. He was clearly touched by the offer and immediately agreed. He reckoned that there would be about six other Americans, he would like to invite, and warned me that they would probably all bring a partner.

The barbecue was a big success. Knowing the English weather, I had hired a marquee, but the weather was good, and we didn't have to use it. The sun shone and several people swam. There were seven Americans other than Rufus and Albert, and five of them bought girlfriends. I don't think it was difficult for an American alone and on a good salary to find a girlfriend in Great Yarmouth. One young man, who came without a girlfriend was introduced as Jim 'Shoulders' Strait. He was very good looking, and all the wives of my neighbours were anxious to meet him. He was a rodeo rider and was nicknamed "Shoulders" after some famous rodeo star. Penny ran the bar for me and seemed to enjoy his attention.

Rufus told me later that he was quite well known in Houston, that he was happily married and a thorough gentleman.

Edward, John and Maurice came from Hobsons. Harry came with his wife and Nigel arrived with a tall lady, who was wearing a revealing summer dress. I hadn't met Harry's wife before, but Dawn was charming and helped me with the barbecue. As the barbecue cooled and we were tidying up, she told me how concerned she was about Nigel. She felt that he was leading her husband's business in a bad direction. Harry, she said, knew this but didn't know what to do about it.

Both the Shell contract and the contract with Grey and Branch went well. Our fishing vessels continued to make losses, but this was more than offset by the profits made from the two contracts with the oil industry. The contract with Grey and Branch had transformed our fortunes and we were blissfully unaware of the drama we were to face that autumn.

Grey and Branch were also bidding on contracts to lay pipes in the northern sector of the North Sea and decided that they would base their northern operations in Peterhead in Scotland. They required someone to set up the base and manage it when pipe-laying operations started the following summer. They consulted Nigel to see if he knew anyone suitable and his first thought was our fleet manager, John Bell. Nigel had John in his pocket for, although we didn't know anything about it, John was already receiving one per cent of our commission, tax free, from the Cayman Islands. So, for Nigel, the possibility of extending his commission scam, with the help of John, to Scotland was very attractive.

Nigel arranged for John to be interviewed and told him that Rufus had been very impressed, and the job was his and that his salary would be almost exactly double the salary he was being paid by us.

Edward and I knew nothing of John's plans, but in July John asked for a meeting. This was rather unusual as John had daily access to Edward at any time, so suspecting something out of the usual, Edward asked me to sit in on the meeting.
John looked very depressed when he entered Edward's office and Edward asked him to sit down.

"What's this all about?" asked Edward kindly.

John explained that whilst he had been happy managing a fleet of trawlers, he was uncomfortable with our entry into the oil industry. He hated being answerable to demanding customers and it was getting him down. He explained that under the Spashetts he had been employed to manage a fleet of fishing vessels and with the entry of Hobsons into the oil support industry his role had completely altered. He would, he said, like to take early retirement. He had been given a 1-year rolling contract by the Spashetts and as his job was now so different from the one, he had been originally hired for, he thought it only fair that Edward should honour the contract, give him a year's salary and let him retire.

Edward and I were both shocked to hear that John was so unhappy in his work. I knew he resented my joining the company and I partly blamed myself for his unhappiness. I don't think this occurred to Edward.

"John, I'm so sorry." replied Edward. "I had no idea you were unhappy. Would you like to take some time off and just reconsider your position? We would hate to lose you."

"No. I have thought about it for some time, and I think it is time for me to retire. Please be as kind as you can."

"Let us just think about it." said Edward. "I'll get back to you shortly."

John stood up and as he offered Edward his hand asked, "May I keep the company car?"

They shook hands and John left the office.

When he was gone, Edward looked at me. "Oh dear!" he said. "What do you make of that?"

We discussed John's position for some time. Edward explained that John had worked for Hobsons for 25 years. He didn't want anyone working for the company who was unhappy and felt that giving him a year's salary was fair. I couldn't really disagree, particularly as I thought that I might well be the source of some of John's unhappiness. Edward decided that John would hand over the day-to-day operations to me and that he would stay officially employed until his 54th birthday, when his departure would be called early retirement. Edward agreed that John would receive one year's salary immediately and would also keep his company car.

We talked about his replacement and Edward suggested that for the time being we should try to share John's work between me and Maurice, our fish salesman. In the meanwhile, I would work more closely with John and familiarise myself further with the skippers and our fishing operations.

I spent the next few weeks in John's office. He was extremely cooperative and helpful. I met all the skippers, and Hobsons' shore staff seemed to accept me as a successor to John. At the end of August, Edward organised a farewell lunch at the Royal Norfolk and Suffolk Yacht Club and all Hobsons' shore staff attended. Edward presented John with a gold Rolex watch and bade him farewell and a happy retirement.

On John's departure, I moved into his office and with the full support of all Hobsons' staff, especially Maurice, coped well with my new responsibilities.

I continued to visit the fish market every morning and tried to be on the quay when we had a trawler sailing. I saw every Skipper when he came into the office to collect his earnings and the ship's husbands encouraged me to go aboard the trawlers when they were in harbour.

It was on one of these visits that one of our team of painters shouted out, "Do you want your house painting?" I didn't know what he meant until the ship's husband told me that John had always had his house painted free by our team of painters.

Chapter 7
Threats

Having banked his retirement money, John kept in close contact with Nigel, who assured him that he would be required to start work in Peterhead in early October, to set up the base to be ready for Grey and Branch when they started pipe-laying operations the following spring. He had not yet been formally appointed by Rufus, but Nigel assured him that he need not worry. He told John that they would both be closely involved when contracts were given out in the new year and hinted that John might be included in a share of any commissions earned from the Peterhead operation.

John began to feel uneasy when Nigel failed to contact him for several days and his calls to Nigel went unanswered. In desperation he telephoned Rufus at the Grey and Branch base.

"I thought I would just make contact." John said. "I am ready for the Peterhead job and just wondered if you would like to see me."

There was a silence. Then Rufus replied, "Hasn't Nigel told you? We've decided to employ a Scot".

"But you can't. I've given up my job and everything."

"I'm sorry." Rufus replied. "Nigel should have told you. We always try and hire a local person, and we've got just the right man".

"You can't do that." John insisted. "You forget that I know that Hobsons are bribing you for the work. If I report you to Houston, you'll be in trouble."

"You bet." Rufus replied nonchalantly and put the phone down.

John was in despair, humiliated, angry and desperate. His first impulse was to contact Nigel, but it took him some time to track him down. He eventually found him in the Railway pub, standing at the bar.

"You bastard! I want to talk to you."

"Not here." Nigel replied, "Let's go outside."

In the carpark outside John squared up to Nigel.

"Are you going to hit me?" Nigel teased as he towered over him.

"What am I going to do?" John pleaded, almost sobbing.

"You shouldn't have left your job until it was certain." Nigel replied as he walked hastily off to his car.

After a sleepless night, John considered Nigel's parting comments. Perhaps he could get his old job back. In desperation he returned to the Hobsons' office the following morning, barged through reception and burst into his old office to find me sitting at his desk. I was talking to Maurice, but ignoring Maurice, he snarled at me.

"How dare you?" John snarled. "I haven't been gone five minutes and you're already at my desk. You jumped up little prat."

This was hardly the approach to get his job back.

"What's up, John?" I was trying to calm him down.

This seemed to infuriate him even further.

"You forget." John replied. "I know what you are up to."

"What do you mean?" I replied.

"I know that you bribed Rufus and Albert to get the contract. You're a crook. This was an honest company until you arrived."

"Come on John. Calm down. Let's talk." I replied.

"I'm not going to quiet down. I'm going to report you to Houston." John said as he made his exit and slammed the door.

I had no doubt what he meant. Houston was the head office of Grey and Branch, and although I had no idea where the ten per cent commission was going, there was a good chance that Rufus and Albert were receiving at least some of it. If their involvement was reported to head office, there was every likelihood that Rufus and Albert would be fired and we would lose the Grey and Branch contract, on which we were relying for survival.

I spent the whole of the day debating whether I should report John's outburst to Edward, but decided I would not worry him and kept John's threat to myself.

Later that day, having threatened me, John burst into Nigel's office and threatened him with exposure.

"You're a dishonest bastard. I know that you are bribing Rufus and Albert to get their business."

"So, what!" Nigel sneered.

"So, What!" John echoed. "I'll tell you so what. I'm going to talk to Houston. I'll tell them what you're doing."

This brought Nigel up short. Grey and Branch's head office might investigate and the repercussions to his commission scam could be disastrous.

Nigel was worried about his dishonesty being reported to Houston. I didn't know it at the time, but Nigel had secured contracts for several supply vessels and anchor handling tugs. In each case he had approached the local managers of the oil companies operating in Yarmouth and told them that he could source vessels and charter them on the understanding that the commission would be five per cent and that two and a half per cent would be paid to them personally into a tax-free account in the Cayman Islands. Many thousands of pounds were at stake.

By chance I had to visit the Grey and Branch site. We were having a minor difficulty with crew changes, which I wanted to discuss. I was immediately ushered into the office that Rufus and Albert shared. Our contract with them meant so much to us that I was always rather apprehensive when I met them, but the barbecue had helped make our meetings less formal. They offered me a coffee and we spent 20 minutes or so talking about the contract. I had come to admire and like them. Although Rufus was the boss, he was always prepared to go to sea and visit the lay barges They were both open and friendly, and I could hardly believe that they were cheating their employer.

During our conversation, they told me that Chuck Branch was coming over from the States to congratulate them on their first season in the North Sea. He was the senior president and major shareholder of Grey and Branch. He was rich and lived in a large house in River Oaks, which Albert explained was the millionaire's row of Houston.

"When are you expecting him?" I asked.

"On Thursday." Rufus replied, "He has business meetings in London and will come down after them."

"Is his wife coming down?" Albert asked.

"No. As far as I know, she's staying on at the Ritz." Rufus replied.

Chapter 8
Modus Operandi

He had worked too long and hard to have his life, career, wealth and reputation ruined by John Bell. He had it all worked out.

He had noticed a short length of heavy chain in the yard; five links that would be easy to handle, yet heavy enough. No one noticed as he put it into the trunk of his car. He then purchased four feet of light chain and two padlocks and drove home. He already had a spare key ring, so in the privacy of his garage, he fastened the key ring to one end of the light chain to form a noose and padlocked the other end of the light chain to the centre link of the heavy chain.

He worked normally for the rest of the day and waited patiently until six that evening before telephoning John.

"John," he said. "I've some very good news."

John grunted.

"I've just been talking to Mark. He really doesn't want you reporting the contract to Houston."

"Why shouldn't I?" asked John.

"He's agreed to give you your job back. He's sure that, if he talks to Edward in the morning, he will be pleased to take you back. There's just one thing he would like to talk to you about tonight."

"What about?" asked John. "I suppose he wants his money back."

"I've arranged for Mark to meet us in his flat at 7 tonight. I think that if I support you, he will let you keep the money."

John was delighted and it was agreed that the two of them would meet up in the car park at Mark's flat just before 7 to discuss a united appeal to Mark for John to keep both his job and his money.

By 7 it was nearly dark, and he waited in the shadows behind one of the poolside changing rooms. He had fastened the heavy chain round his neck like a yoke, with the other end of the light chain forming a noose, which he held in both hands. The padlock was tucked safely into the palm of his right hand.

John parked his car, and as he got out, he heard, "Hello John. Just here a minute. I want to talk tactics."

As John stepped towards the pool, the noose was slipped quickly over his neck and pulled tight. The padlock clicked shut. John struggled but he was pushed firmly towards the pool. There was a splash as the heavy chain was thrown into the pool and a larger splash as John followed.

Satisfied with his work, the murderer walked calmly to Mark's flat, pushed the padlock keys into his letter box, returned to his car and drove off.

Chapter 9
The Swimming Pool

Looking back, I still find it strange that, as I left for work that Tuesday morning, I had no premonition, and was so unaware, of the tragedy that had taken place. I suppose I was so used to my routine and so intent on getting to work on time that I failed to see the significance of the signs that might have alerted me.

Although I left for work far earlier than the postman delivered the mail, I always checked my mailbox. Occasionally I found some leaflet, or the Parish Magazine, that had been delivered the night before, but normally the box was empty. On this morning I found two pairs of padlock keys. They were strange keys, with Master written on them. I did not recognise them but put them in my trouser pocket and, as I walked to my car, vaguely wondered why they were in my mailbox. My parking place, like all the others, was along one side of the pool behind the changing rooms. There were six parking places and four additional spaces marked with a V for visitors. From my space I could see the swimming pool between the two poolside changing rooms and was surprised to see a shoe lying beside the pool. It was a gentleman's brown slip-on shoe and I vaguely wondered how it came to be there. There was also a car parked in one of the visitors' parking spaces. It was vaguely familiar, but I was in a hurry to get to work and backed out of my space and drove off.

Scott Randall, the gardener, arrived at Brooke House at 8.30. He came every other Tuesday and would have started earlier, but the residents had complained about the noise of his lawnmower, and he was not able to start until then. He parked his truck and trailer in the three free visitors' parking bays and his assistant David helped him unload the mower. Scott set about mowing the lawn that ran up and down each side of the drive and David started to sweep up any leaves or debris that had accumulated round the pool. As he approached the pool, he noticed a brown slip-on shoe, so he carefully picked it up and put it on the bench in the male changing room. He had not been sweeping long before he detected something at the bottom of the deep end of the pool. He looked closer. It was a body. He rushed to get Scott and they both peered into the pool. Scott ran to the house and ringing all the doorbells entered the first flat that answered and dialled 999.

The call was taken by Sergeant Brock, who immediately contacted PC Ian Greystone, the local bobby whose beat encompassed Oulton Road and Brooke House. He jumped in his panda car and raced to Brooke House. Scott and David showed him the submerged body, and PC Greystone told them to get well away from the pool. He contacted Sergeant Brock to confirm the finding of a body, reported that divers would be required to recover the body, and began to secure the site with the police tape and poles that he had in his car.

Within 15 minutes Detective Sergeant Slight was on the scene, shortly followed by a team of divers and forensic investigators. The body was recovered and quickly identified, from his wallet, as being John Bell. PC Greystone was confined to watching procedures until Sergeant Slight told him to pick up a lady PC and go to Mr. Bell's house to inform his wife of her husband's death. PC Greystone would have preferred to be armed with a bit more information before talking to Mrs. Bell but realised that procedures were in place to ensure that the widow didn't hear of her husband's demise from the press. At the Police Station PC Diana Lufkin was on duty. She was older than Greystone and suggested that she did the talking. PC Greystone was amazed at how quickly Mrs. Bell reacted to the news. There was no stunned amazement, just instant grief as she broke down in tears. Diana Lufkin was fantastically sympathetic and comforting and Greystone was confined to making tea.

Ian Greystone had not been long in the force. He had wanted to be a policeman from the age of ten, largely because he had admired his uncle Ernest Greystone, who was an officer with the Great Yarmouth Police Force. In fact, he had considered applying to join the Yarmouth Police until his uncle, who had now risen to the rank of Superintendent, dissuaded him. Uncle Ernest felt that it would be a disadvantage for his nephew, bearing the same name, to be under his command and he didn't feel that a small force like that of Great Yarmouth could last much longer.

Chapter 10
Investigations

Finding the body held down with heavy chain in the deep end of the swimming pool, with frothing round the mouth and nose, Detective Sergeant Slight didn't have to be a genius to assume that the cause of John Bell's demise was death by drowning. When he reported to Detective Inspector Roper, he was able to tell him that it looked as if John had weighted himself down and thrown himself into the pool to take his own life. DI Roper was an experienced officer, nearing retirement and looking for a quiet life, but he instructed Detective Sergeant Slight to interview John's wife and his employer to investigate whether he had shown signs of stress or depression.

Sergeant Slight located PC Diana Lufkin and together they drove to Mrs. Bell's house.

"How was she?" asked Sergeant Slight.

"How do you think?" Diana replied. "She'd just been told that her husband was dead."

"Don't get narky with me." Slight replied. "Just tell me what happened."

"She completely broke down. We did our best and Greystone made tea while I comforted her."

"Does she have any family?" asked Slight.

"No. Well no children anyway. Her best friend lives next door and we got her over and she said she would look after her until I returned. I explained that she would have to answer questions from someone more senior."

"Do you think I should ask the questions?" Slight asked. "Or might they be better coming from you?"

"That depends on whether we can let her neighbour stay during the interview. If we can let her stay and comfort her, I could ask the questions. That might be better."

They agreed to let the neighbour stay and that Diana would ask the questions.

Diana's approach was sympathetic and gentle and Mrs. Bell, although tearful, was only too pleased to cooperate. It became clear that only a few weeks earlier, her husband had been very excited about a new job with an American company working out of Great Yarmouth. He had discussed it with his wife as it required him to work in Peterhead. He would be away for nearly a year, and, after that, the job was largely seasonal. His accommodation in Peterhead would be paid for as would all travel costs both for him and his wife. She could visit as often as she liked, and the pay was double what he was earning with Hobsons.

Mrs. Bell had some reservations, but John was so set on the new job that she encouraged him to take it.

It was some weeks later that John told her that the job had fallen through and that he had already left his old job at Hobsons. He was angry, distraught and depressed.

Diana's final question was, "Did you think that John was so depressed that he was suicidal?"

Mrs. Bell sobbed and after a long pause she replied, "No. I didn't think he'd do that." She broke down completely, and Diana stopped the questions and helped the neighbour comfort her.

When they returned to the police station, they jointly compiled a full report and Sergeant Slight presented it to Inspector Roper. Sergeant Slight had a reputation at the station for always being right, until he was wrong. In fact, behind his back he was called 'Slight is right.'

"It looks like suicide." Slight commented.

"Interview someone from his work." Roper ordered. "From his old job and from the one that he hoped to go to."

By now it was late afternoon. Both he and Diana had failed to obtain the name or address of the potential new employer. Slight knew that they were American and based in Great Yarmouth. He also knew that he would have to contact the Great Yarmouth Constabulary before he could question someone on their patch. He would get Diana to contact Mrs. Bell again to find out the name and address of the new employer and interview them tomorrow, but for now he had had enough.

Slight was getting ready to go home when he received a call from the pathologist dealing with John Bell's remains saying that they had lost a shoe. Would he see whether it was still in the pool. Slight had no intention of driving over to Brooke House so ordered Greystone to see if he could find the missing shoe.

Until now I had no idea of what had occurred at my pool, but, at about the same time as PC Ian Greystone was receiving his instructions from DS Slight, Maurice burst into my office.

"Have you seen this?" he exclaimed pointing at an article in the Eastern Evening News. "John is dead. They seem to think it's suicide. In your pool."

I took the paper from him. Sure, enough there was a brief article under the headline – "Man found dead in pool." It explained that police had been called to a private swimming pool at Brooke House, Oulton, where the body of a man had been found. It identified the man as John Bell aged 53. Next of kin had been informed.

"Why did you say suicide?" I asked.

"Well what else could it have been?" Maurice replied.

"It could have been an accident."

As I drove home from the office, I was hardly able to believe that the newspaper report was true, but when I turned into the driveway of Brooke House, a police panda car followed me down the drive and parked in one of the visitors' bays. I noticed the police tape round the pool and immediately recognised that the car I had seen in the visitors' parking space was John Bell's company car, the one that he had kept when he retired.

As I got out of my car, PC Greystone got out of his panda car. He looked at me and asked,

"Do you live here, Sir?"

When I replied that I did, he got out his notebook and asked if I would help him with his enquiries. I told him that I was pleased to do so, and Greystone noted down my name, address and telephone number.

"Would you please wait there a minute?" he asked and walked towards the pool and peered into the deep end.

"What are you looking for? I asked, "I may be able to help."

"I'm looking for a shoe." he replied.

"Yes. I thought you might be. It was on the edge of the pool when I left for work this morning."

Greystone looked sharply at me, but his attitude changed. He became much less formal, and although he continued to make notes, he engaged me in conversation, rather than questioning me.

"You can't cross the tape, Sir, but would you show me where you saw the shoe?"

He collected a traffic cone from his car and following my instructions, placed it exactly where the shoe had been. He took a polaroid photograph.

"I suppose he must have tripped. Did he hit his head when he fell in?" I asked.

"Did you know the victim?" Greystone asked.

"Yes. I used to work with him. It must have been an accident."

"How do you know who **he** is?" He replied.

I explained that I had read of John Bell's death in the newspaper, and Greystone appeared rather surprised.

"It wasn't an accident." Greystone confided. "He had padlocked a heavy chain round his neck. We think it was suicide. Do you know of any reason why he would take his own life?"

Had John committed suicide? Could it be true? I'd taken his job. A job he'd had for many years. I knew he blamed me, perhaps that was why he had chosen to kill himself in my pool. Then I remembered the shoe. It must have been John's shoe, and I thought to myself; what person, however stressed, takes off one shoe before committing suicide?

I think Greystone thought the same because he said thoughtfully, "Perhaps it wasn't suicide?"

"Who discovered the body?" I asked.

"It was the gardeners. They dialled 999."

"Perhaps they saw the shoe before they discovered the body and put it somewhere safe. Have you looked everywhere?"

Greystone rather resented my question but immediately looked in the changing room. Without saying anything he walked to his car, collected an evidence bag and came out of the changing room with what was obviously the shoe.

"Found it." he confirmed. "Is there anything more that you can tell me, Sir?"

He seemed surprised when I told him that the Ford Granada in the bay next to him belonged to John Bell.

"Do you know the registration number?"

"No." I replied. "But I am sure that it's his."

Greystone noted down the registration number and as he did so, my thoughts went to the four padlock keys that I had found in my mailbox.

"Did you say padlocked?" I asked as I fetched the four keys out of my pocket.
"I found these in my mailbox before I went to work this morning."

Greystone was not sure how to respond, but he examined the keys before taking a small envelope from his pocket and asking me to drop the keys into the envelope. As I did so, I realised, with some concern, that my fingerprints would be all over them.

As I walked to my flat, I realised that I had probably persuaded Greystone that John's death was not suicide and was probably murder. I had no idea as to who had killed him, but I began to wonder whether the motive might have been something to do with the ten per cent commission that we were paying Bark and Company. After all, John had burst into my office and threatened to expose Hobsons to Grey and Branch's headquarters in Houston. If he had threatened Rufus and Albert, or Nigel and Harry, they might have reacted rather differently and wanted to silence him. It seemed far-fetched but I also realised that, when Greystone reported our conversation to Sergeant Slight, there was a very good chance that he would regard me as the prime suspect.

Chapter 11
The Ritz

I had one advantage over the police, I knew that I had not harmed John, let alone killed him. Before the police started suspecting me, I realised that I was in a unique position to make my own investigations. I knew that Chuck Branch was in London, staying at the Ritz with his wife. I felt sure that a conversation with him would be helpful. Without telling anyone, I decided to drive to London.

I spent the night at a small hotel near Gants Hill and drove into London the following morning. I parked in a car park in Arlington Street and arrived at the Ritz shortly after 10. When I approached the enquiry desk, there was a tall slender lady talking to the head porter. She had an American accent and was asking him what time the changing of the guard took place at Buckingham Palace. As she stepped away from the desk, I asked the head porter if Mr. Branch was staying. The tall American turned.

"Who's asking?" asked the lady.

I introduced myself.

"I'm Doreen Branch, Chuck's wife." she said.

I explained that I was from Lowestoft and that we had three ships working for his company and that I had just come to pay my respects and discuss a minor operational matter.

"I'm not sure he'll be able to help you on that," Doreen replied kindly. "He leaves all that to Rufus. He's at a meeting this morning and won't be back till four."

"Thank you." I replied.

"Besides," Doreen continued. "I'm just getting a taxi to Buckingham Palace to watch them changing the guard."

"Please don't do that."

Doreen looked startled. "Why not?" she asked.

"It's a lovely day and it's only a short walk from here. You could be there by the time you got a taxi."

"But…." started Doreen. She was clearly going to say that she did not know the way.

"I'll show you the way. But we better be quick it's twenty to eleven and it starts at 11."

Doreen didn't hesitate. She slipped into her expensive coat and said, "Okay. Let's go."

We walked along the Ritz's colonnade and turned left down some steps into Green Park.

"That's Buckingham Palace, just over there." I said pointing straight ahead.

As we walked, I became very aware that I did not know London as well as I should. There was a sign saying that the building on our left was Spencer House.

I said, "That must belong to Earl Spencer, but I don't think he lives there."

"No." Doreen replied, "They live at Althorp." and she pronounced it correctly.

I did know Lancaster House, but only because I had worked there as a waiter, and I was able to tell her it was owned by the government and used for government hospitality.

When we reached Buckingham Palace, we were able to find a place near the railings with a good view, and Doreen seemed to enjoy the spectacle. The old guard finally marched off to the Wellington barracks, and I pointed out the Mall and St James' Park. Doreen explained that she had only arrived the previous day and had not been to London before, so I suggested that we return to the Ritz and that I would collect my car from the car park and give her a quick tour in my car.

My battered old Ford Anglia looked a bit incongruous outside the Ritz, but I had pushed the passenger seat right back and the porter ushered Doreen into the car, receiving a note for his pains. We drove along Piccadilly, where I pointed out the Park Lane Hotel, which was not in Park Lane. I waved northward to indicate Park Lane and Hyde Park and told her that Grosvenor House, the Dorchester and the new Hilton were on Park Lane. We went down Constitution Hill, The Mall, through Admiralty Arch, passed the National gallery, round Trafalgar Square, down Whitehall to see the Cenotaph, Downing Street, Big Ben, the Houses of Parliament and Westminster Abbey, wriggled through to Victoria Street, the Roman Catholic Cathedral, on to Eaton Square, Sloane Square and ended up at the back of Harrods, where I parked.

"I thought you would like to end up at Harrods."

She grinned and said, "You bet." But she looked at her watch. It was now nearly 2 in the afternoon, and I had forgotten that she might be hungry. I suggested a small restaurant in Beauchamp Place and insisted that I pay, so we ate there before spending an hour in Harrods.

When we returned to the Ritz, we found Chuck in the Rivoli bar having a coffee and Doreen introduced us. She had clearly enjoyed her day, and as she left us alone, she said, "Be nice to this young man."

Chuck offered me a coffee, which I accepted, and I started to tell him that we had three boats on charter to him at Yarmouth, that we got on very well with Rufus and Albert and that the contract was going well.

"What's the problem?" he asked.

I was very frank and told him that we were paying a ten per cent commission, when the normal would have been two and a half and I was concerned as to where the commission was going.

"Do you know anything about it?" I asked.

Chuck smiled. "Rufus and Albert have worked for me for many years in many parts of the world. I trust them completely. From time to time, they accept gifts and inducements to betray me, but they never do. They always tell me about them."

"Do you know about the commission?"

"Of course," Chuck replied. "I'm not sure that I have got the detail quite right, but Rufus and Albert are getting two per cent each, paid into an account in the Cayman Islands. Two and a half goes to a marine survey company, two and a half to some guy called Nigel and one per cent to one of your guys. Did you know that?"

I was astonished and clearly showed it.

"You didn't know, did you? That's interesting. Rufus didn't think you knew. That's why we didn't make him our Peterhead manager. We thought that if he would screw you, he might screw us."

This was all news to me, but it was clear who he was talking about. John had clearly negotiated his payoff from us thinking he was going to work for Grey and Branch. I thanked Chuck for the information and, as I got up to go, Doreen came into the cocktail bar, so I was able to say goodbye to them both.

As I headed towards the city, it occurred to me to call in at Stewart Offshore and talk to Tony White. Stewarts were well respected agents who worked in offshore oil. I just caught Tony before he left the office, and we went round the corner for a beer. I asked him some general questions about Great Yarmouth.

"Don't talk to me about Yarmouth," Tony grumbled. "We can't get any work there. Some marine surveyor has got it all stitched up, by backhanders so they say."

Tony had told me enough.

Chapter 12
Locked Up

When Greystone left me after our conversation at Brooke House, he was convinced that John's death was probably murder. He was unsure what to do with his knowledge, but as he had done many times before, he telephoned his uncle, Superintendent Ernest Greystone, at his home in Yarmouth.

"Come over, and talk." Ernest suggested.

Half an hour later he was sitting comfortably in Ernest's office with a Double Diamond in hand, relating his suspicions. He explained the whole case to his uncle, including the new evidence about the missing shoe and the padlock keys.

"They were very odd keys," he explained. "They had 'Master' written on them. I've never seen keys like them."

"What's the problem?" asked his uncle.

Greystone explained to his uncle that both Sergeant Slight and DI Roper seemed to be happy with a suicide verdict and were reluctant to investigate John's death as a murder. He doubted that even with the new evidence regarding the shoes and the keys they would change their minds.

"I shouldn't worry about that," his uncle replied. "Inspector Roper is no idiot, and he is always very thorough."

"By the way, which Lowestoft company is involved?"

"It's a fishing company called Hobsons. They have been in Lowestoft a long time and are very well respected."

He went on to explain that Hobsons had managed to charter some of their ships to the oil industry.

"That will be in Yarmouth, I expect," Ernest was thinking out loud. "In that case the Lowestoft force will probably have to interview someone in Yarmouth. They will need our consent for that. I may be able to get involved. By the way, I don't think you should mention this conversation to your superiors at Lowestoft. Leave it to me."

The following morning Detective Sergeant Slight asked Diana to return to Mrs. Bell's house and ask her whether she could remember the name of the company that had offered her husband a job. Mrs. Bell had no idea but told Diana that they laid pipe in the North Sea and that they would be operating out of Peterhead the following year.

Slight was not happy and seemed to blame Diana for her failure to provide a name, but Diana responded by suggesting that he conduct his interview with Hobsons first. So shortly before midday, Detective Sergeant Slight together with PC Diana Lufkin walked into Hobsons' reception area and asked to speak to the manager. Maurice greeted them and explained that I had not turned up for work that day and asked if he could help. He suggested that they hold the meeting in the boardroom so that they would not be disturbed.

They established quickly that John Bell had managed the Hobsons fleet for many years and had only left recently. Slight asked whether John had left on good terms and whether he was happy about his departure. Maurice explained that John had enjoyed an excellent retirement party and received a very nice watch. He thought John was happy about his early retirement and had been surprised when he had returned to the office to accuse Mark of bribing Grey and Branch to obtain charters for three of their stern trawlers and threatening to report the bribery to their head office in Houston.

"What do you mean, bribes?" Slight demanded.

"I've no idea." Maurice replied honestly.

Slight asked why I was not in the office and whether there was anyone more senior he could interview. Maurice explained that the managing director was Edward Utting and that Ivan was the company secretary. Maurice knocked on Edward's door and introduced DS Slight and PC Lufkin to Edward. Edward lifted his internal phone and immediately asked Ivan to join him in his office. When Ivan entered, Edward came from behind his desk and sat together with the other three round the coffee table.

Edward dismissed Maurice with a "Thank you, Maurice."

Slight was forthright.

"I have received information," he began, "that you are paying inducements to Grey and Branch so that they charter three of your vessels. Is this true?"

Edward looked at Ivan and said, "Ivan, explain exactly to detective Sergeant Slight what we are doing."

Ivan explained that Hobson's invoiced Grey and Branch every calendar month for the charter of each ship. He explained that Bark and Company had arranged the charters and were entitled to a commission. Hobson's received an invoice from Bark and Company for their commission, which was paid monthly.

Ivan glanced at Edward. He was wondering if he should go further, but Edward chipped in saying, "Perhaps I ought to tell you that the commission is considerably higher than we would normally expect to pay."

Slight wanted to know exactly what percentage was normal and the commission Hobsons was actually paying. When this had been established, Slight asked whether there was anything else about the commission payment that was unusual.

Edward replied as if it were quite normal by saying, "Of course we pay the commission to Bark and Company's account in the Caymen islands."

Slight scribbled in his notebook and asked, "Who is Mark Stretton? What position in the company does he hold?"

Edward explained that I had taken over from John Bell.

"How long has he been with the company?" asked Slight.

"About eight months." Edward replied.

"Is he a shareholder in the company?"

"Oh yes." replied Edward in as matter of fact a tone as he could muster. He was dreading the next question.

"How many shares does he hold?"

"He owns ninety per cent of the company." Edward answered casually.

Slight scribbled in his notebook.

"Are you aware that the deceased accused Mark Stretton of bribing the staff at Grey and Branch in order to obtain the contract."

Edward looked genuinely surprised but before he could answer, Slight continued, "John Bell threatened Stretton that he would report the Grey and Branch staff to their head office."

Neither Edward nor Ivan knew anything about this, and Slight continued, "Would the loss of the contract impact significantly on Hobson's profits?"

"Somewhat." Edward replied cautiously.

Detective Sergeant Slight and PC Diana Lufkin left. Their next visit would be to Grey and Branch in Great Yarmouth, but they were obliged to contact the Yarmouth constabulary to obtain permission to interview someone in the Yarmouth area. Slight contacted the duty officer at Yarmouth. He seemed to be expecting the call and after briefly explaining the reason for the request, the duty officer agreed and asked whether Superintendent Greystone could accompany them. It was agreed that Supt. Greystone would make the appointment for three that afternoon.

In the event Slight decided to go alone and not take Diana and he met up with Superintendent Greystone in Grey and Branch's car park. Sergeant Slight was irked that so senior an officer should have decided to attend his interview and was relieved when Supt. Greystone insisted that Slight should conduct the interview and that he would only observe. They were shown into the office shared by Rufus and Albert and explained the reason for their visit. Slight asked how the charter payments to Hobson's were paid. Whereupon Rufus picked up his phone and asked their accountant to join them. The accountant explained the procedure and, when prompted by Slight, confirmed that there was nothing unusual in this procedure or any of the payments.

The two policemen left Grey and Branch and Superintendent Greystone suggested that they both had a cup of tea in the nearby café. Greystone, who had listened intently to Slight, asked whether he thought John's death had been suicide. Slight was completely dismissive of this idea and explained to the Inspector that he had discovered that Mark Stretton owned ninety per cent of Hobson's and had bribed Grey and Branch to hire three of their largest vessels. He explained that their fishing fleet was making losses and that the only way the company was surviving was through the charter to Grey and Branch. He continued to explain that John, having lost his job, had discovered that bribery was involved and threatened Mark that he would report his dishonesty to Grey and Branch's head office. Slight was convinced that Mark had enticed John to his house, met him in the car park and thrown him into the swimming pool weighed down with a heavy chain. The keys to the padlocks, used to fasten the chains, had been discovered on Mark's person. Mark had now fled the scene and was clearly in hiding. After consulting Inspector Roper, he had arranged for two policemen to wait for Mark at his home and arrest him should he return.

Inspector Greystone asked whether Inspector Roper had commented on the case and Greystone was amused to learn that he had told Slight that there was no problem in arresting Mark, but that he was not to be charged until he had interviewed Mark himself.

"Can I help in any way?" asked Inspector Greystone.

"I don't see how, Sir." Slight answered rather too quickly.

"I just wondered about the keys. Did they look new?"

"Oh, yes," replied Slight, "I imagine they were bought specifically for the job."

"Of course, if we could tie the purchase of these keys to Mark Stretton, it would be crucial evidence," the superintendent suggested. "Would you mind if I made enquiries at the Yarmouth hardware shops to see if any of them sold the padlocks to Mark?"

Slight was surprised that so senior an officer should volunteer for so menial a task but could see no harm and willingly agreed.

That evening PC Greystone again visited his uncle at his house in Yarmouth and as they sat having a beer in the inspector's old-fashioned office, they reviewed the case of John's drowning. Young Greystone was thankful that Slight had accepted that John's death had not been suicide, and Uncle Ernest told him that Slight was now convinced that Mark was the killer. Ian told his uncle about his meeting with Mark at the swimming pool. In his view Mark had not behaved like a guilty person.

"I have known many criminals who do not behave like guilty people." Ernest responded, "But, I agree with you. There isn't a shred of evidence against him, unless we can prove that the padlock keys were his or bought by him. I've persuaded Slight to let me investigate whether the keys were purchased in the Yarmouth area. I have an idea."

As Ian was talking to his uncle, I was driving home from London. By now it was rush-hour, and my journey was slow. It was nearly ten o'clock when I parked outside my flat. There was a police car in one of the visitors' parking spaces and as I got out of my car, two uniformed officers approached me, asked my name and told me to accompany them for questioning regarding the death of John Bell. It was clear that I didn't have any option, so I climbed into the back of the car next to one of the officers. At the police station, I was processed and led off to a cell. I was told that I would be interviewed in the morning and the cell door banged shut. I looked round my cell. There was no toilet, just a galvanized bucket, and no basin. For a bed there was a low concrete slab, grooved to resemble a draining board. I guessed that this was the accommodation for drunks, who were likely to urinate.

At six in the morning, after an almost sleepless night, the door opened, and I was served a mug of tea and a ham sandwich.

Fortunately, although I did not know it, Superintendent Greystone was pursuing his hunch. His nephew had told him that the keys had "Master" written on them and although he was familiar with Squire, Yale, Union and Chubb, he had never heard of "Master." There were so many Americans in Yarmouth these days that he wondered whether "Master" might be the name of an American padlock and the only hardware store that was likely to stock American padlocks was R. J. Pryce & Co., which was managed by an American.

There are numerous cases of criminals who, like Neville Heath, give themselves away through stupidity or arrogance. In his case, he took a lady to his hotel room, murdered her and fled, completely forgetting that he had signed the hotel register with his real name and address. Inspector Greystone had heard all the tales but even he was surprised by what he discovered at R. J. Pryce. They stocked Master padlocks and when he asked whether they had sold any recently, they were able to confirm that they had sold two padlocks and a length of chain on the previous Monday. As they were trade only, the order for the two padlocks had been on a Bark and Company order book. The signature was indecipherable, but the field was considerably narrowed.

Inspector Greystone knew that his first duty was to inform Slight, but he had known Harry Bark for many years, even before he had set up as a marine surveyor. Then he had been a superintendent engineer for Everards, the shipping company, and although they were not close friends, their paths had crossed on several social and civic occasions, and they were on Christian name terms. Greystone liked Harry and decided to give him a visit. He first went to Harry's office, where he was informed that Harry had gone home early the previous day as he was not feeling well. He had not arrived at work that morning and the office had assumed that he was still unwell. Greystone decided to visit him at home and when he rang the bell, Harry's wife, Dawn, answered.

"Is Harry in?" Greystone asked.

"He's in, but he's in bed," Dawn replied. "I'm sure he'll see you, but may I talk to you first."

She led him into their living room.

"I think Harry's on the verge of a nervous breakdown," she confided. "I don't know why, but he's very upset and seems frightened."

As Dawn said this, Harry came into the room.

"Oh! Ernest am I pleased to see you!" he was almost crying.

Ernest suggested that Dawn and Harry sit down and explain the problem and when they were settled, Harry said.

"I think Nigel has murdered John."

Harry talked for some time. He was clearly relieved to tell the truth. He had no direct evidence that Nigel had killed John, but he was dreadfully afraid that he had. He told Ernest how he had fallen under Nigel's influence and when he finished, he cried with relief. Dawn hugged him, and he cried even more.

Greystone listened intently and then to Harry's obvious surprise asked how many people at Bark and Company were authorised to place orders on behalf of the company, and whether they all had order books. Harry explained that only three people had that authority, the office manageress called Mary, Nigel and himself.

Supt. Greystone had heard enough. He decided to go to Lowestoft and see Sergeant Slight and when he arrived, he suggested that they should both talk to Inspector Roper in his office. Greystone was very diplomatic. He explained that Sergeant Slight had discovered that bribery was involved in the granting of charters of vessels to the oil industry and that on Slight's advice he had investigated the sale of the two padlocks. He had reason to believe that a Nigel Mann had purchased the padlocks on Monday from R.J.Pryce on a Bark and Co. order book.

Greystone suggested that a warrant be obtained to search Nigel's home, place of work and car to find his order book. He looked at his watch.

"If I ring the clerk of the court at Yarmouth, I am pretty sure that he can get the magistrates to sit before two o'clock. Percy Trett will almost certainly turn out during his lunch hour as will either Oliver Payne or Graham Plant. We could have a search warrant by two thirty."

Inspector Roper responded immediately. "I think we should search his house and car simultaneously. Slight, can you get together nine or ten officers and brief them so that we can carry out the search as soon as the search warrant is in our hands."

"Of course." Slight answered enthusiastically as he jumped to his feet and left the office.

"May I use your phone?" Greystone asked Roper.

At two forty-five the order book was found in the glove compartment of Nigel's car. The carbon copy matched the order for padlocks and chain in every respect and Nigel was arrested within minutes.

I knew I was innocent of any crime, but it was still a great relief when shortly after three in the afternoon I was taken from my cell and without any explanation reunited with my belongings and released. The first thing I saw as I walked out of the police station door was Penny walking towards me. We both ran to each other and hugged. The hug turned into a kiss. A kiss we will always remember.

Chapter 13
Transition

We continued to work for Grey and Branch for six years, two out of Yarmouth, two out of Peterhead and two out of Bombay in India. The commission dropped to two and a half per cent and was paid into Harry's company account at the Yarmouth branch of Barclays bank.

In 1976 Robert Fubini approached us. He worked for Clarksons, a huge London shipbroking company. Robert specialised in the sale of fishing vessels. The Ministry of Defence had asked him to purchase four large fishing vessels for conversion to training ships for the RNVR. They were to be based at Cardiff, Swansea, Liverpool and Bristol. He knew that we had twelve stern trawlers that would be suitable for conversion and asked if we would be prepared to sell four to the Navy.

At the time we were doubtful about selling off our newest and best vessels particularly as we could see various roles for them in the exploration and production stages of North Sea oil development. At the last minute the Ministry of Defence decided to charter them rather than buy them, so we converted four vessels and chartered them initially for a period of two years that was extended to four.

Over the years all our other fishing vessels were converted to work in the oil industry. However, Edward and I were very aware that, although the North Sea was important, the offshore oil industry was a growing worldwide business that would require specialist vessels, not converted fishing vessels. Hobsons was now very profitable, so we embarked on a programme of building oil rig supply vessels.

We changed the name of the company to Hobson Marine Limited and all the ships had a Hobson prefix such as the Hobson Mariner, or Hobson Endeavour. They were all diesel electric and of the same Norwegian design so that spare parts were common to the whole fleet. Over the years we built nine supply vessels; they were almost sister ships. They were successful.

Maurice remained fleet manager, but when our engineering superintendent retired, we appointed an excellent engineer with worldwide experience. We also employed Keith Shannon, an experienced chartering manager, responsible for worldwide sales.

When Ivan Dannock retired, we replaced him with an experienced qualified accountant called Ken Jenner. With his arrival, it was time to change the structure of the company. Edward remained chairman. I called myself deputy chairman. Maurice became managing director and Ken became finance director.

As for my personal life, Penny and I got married in St. Margarets Church, Lowestoft in 1977 and our first child, a little boy, who we called Edward Myles, was born in 1979. Elizabeth May was born two years later.

Over the years we sold several of the older fishing vessels. We had written these vessels down to nothing in our books, but inflation ensured that we sold them all for more than their original price. The transition from a fishing company to an offshore supply vessel company was completed in 1986 when Spain joined the EEC. The Spanish fishing industry saw this as a huge opportunity.

They required more fishing vessels, but they had to have a Common Fishery Policy licence. We had almost forgotten that our ships still had this valuable licence, which we were allowed to resurrect. Over the next year or two the Spanish industry bought all our fishing vessels, sometimes arriving at Lowestoft with the money in cash in a suitcase.

Chapter 14
More Myles

Quite out of the blue I received a telephone call from Myles Horton-McDowd.

He greeted me as if we had spoken the previous week. "It's Myles here. How are you?"

"Hello, is that Mr. Horton-McDowd?" I replied, although I already knew it was. I would recognise his voice anywhere.

"I won't beat about the bush." Myles continued. "I've got a little proposition, which might interest you."

I was understandably cautious, but in the end, I agreed to meet him. He suggested the Great Eastern Hotel and we agreed a date and time.

When we met, he explained that under the new Financial Services Act, it was possible for individuals, liable to pay tax, to roll over their liability by investing in an unquoted company such as Hobson Marine. He had no personal involvement with the scheme, but a friend of his had asked him whether he knew a company that would appeal to potential investors. Not unnaturally, so he said, he had thought of Hobsons. It transpired that he had obtained a copy of our accounts ever since he had sold me ninety per cent of the company for £20. He congratulated me on how well I had done and admired the current position of the company and its potential.

"I just have two questions for you." Myles continued. "Would you consider selling and if so, may I introduce you to my friend?"

Until recently I had pressed ahead with Hobsons Marine in the certain, but false, knowledge that I only had £20 at stake, but since marrying and having children I had become more aware of the risks I was taking. The new supply ships were costing six million pounds each, and I had come to realise that the oil industry was subject to worldwide political and financial vagaries.

I will not bore you with the details, but within six months, with the agreement of Edward, we had sold the company.

Penny and I considered what we would do for the future. We had no illusions about the hotel industry, but we both still wanted some involvement. We agreed that any hotel would have to be of sufficient size to be able to support a full-time manager. In the end we bought a luxury hotel in Surrey. We acquired the hotel for about ten per cent of our net proceeds from the sale of Hobson Marine. We set aside ten per cent for improvements, and we invested the remainder via a very reputable advisor. I was amused to discover that one of his investments was HMIT.

We have lived happily ever after.

Milton Keynes UK
Ingram Content Group UK Ltd.
UKHW040950140324
439439UK00001B/40